I0520859

Printed in the United States of America

First Printing: Oct 2016

Typeset in Garamond 11pt

Published by: Asgard Studios
Ottawa, Canada
www.asgard-studios.com

ISBN: 978-1927646649

Hrymar™, **Illar**™ , **Ysgar**™, and **Tribes of Yggdrasil**™ are Trademarks of Hugh B. Long

Library and Archives Canada Cataloguing in Publication

Pending

TUESDAY, APRIL 9TH, 3478

MY NAME'S DICK WILSON. I had two goals on the morning of April 9th, 3478; grab a cup of coffee and stop a serial killer at our retirement home. I did neither.

You ever have one of those mornings where it feels like the whole Universe has gone to shit and all you want to do is curl up in bed with a cup of coffee? Yeah, it was one of those mornings.

Of course I'll explain the serial killer statement. Yes, and the retirement home. One thing at a time.

Sunday, April 7th, 3478

TWO DAYS EARLIER

I WOKE up at 6:00am like I always do. My plan for the day was simple: I would go for breakfast, after which I'd play chess with my friend Sheldon. Then we would do some group activities, followed by lunch, followed by more scheduled activities, followed by dinner, followed by tv, followed by bed. It's a routine. I like routines. At my age it's all that's left.

I live at a place called the Fairfield Arms Relativistic & Time Traveler's Sanctuary. Yes, that spells FARTTS. We at the Sanctuary were self-proclaimed Old Farts—we owned it!

Guys like me were designated RR—relativity refugees. I'd been on the first long-distance missions to explore Rigel. We flew at a constant 1 g to provide the crew artificial gravity. The journey took 13 years, meanwhile, over 914 years passed for the folks on Earth—that pesky relativity thingy. But hey, we knew that going in.

The annoying part was that some geniuses had invented time travel and jump-drive in the intervening nine centuries. RR folks like me were contacted and recruited for the Space-Time Defense program. It gave us a chance to keep working and belong to a community that was essentially *atemporal*.

Why the Sanctuary? Where the Hell else are you going to dump a bunch of worn out misfits that are displaced in time, disconnected with modern culture, and generally dangerous? This is the pasture for old hackers, codebreakers, assassins, and the like. Our previous employer, Space-Time Defense, really didn't appreciate critical assets wandering around dribbling secrets and such.

The one thing we could never do is go back in time.

Guys who hopped around in time—time travelers—became temporal refugees—TRs. They were also prevented from ever going backward. Physically, it was possible. Legally, absolutely forbidden—with one exception—the Sanctuary. When us RRs and TRs were ready to retire, we got sent here. The Sanctuary is located on a planet unknown to us residents, and, we were told, resides millions of years in the past; though I still calculate time from my last posting. Apparently this is a safe place for us to muck about—a planet that will never evolve complex organisms, but has all the natural resources we need to live well.

So here we are, doing time, so to speak. Could be worse, I suppose—we could run out of coffee. Gods forbid! Then a serial killer would be the least of the Sanctuary's problems. "Mr. Wilson?" I heard a woman's voice from my open door —it was Dr. Calliope Chopra, my new cultural therapist. It was her job to help manage any cross-cultural conflicts between patients of different times and places. Most of us were from within the same century, but a lot could, and did, change in a 100 years..

I was still lying in bed and rolled over to look at my clock

—it read 6:08am. I didn't have to be at breakfast for 22 minutes. Why the Hell was she up my ass so early?

"Richard? Can you hear me?" she asked, as she walked toward my bed. Nobody but my mother had ever called me Richard. Was that some sort of shrink tactic?

I sat up, flipped off the blanket and stood up to meet her. She gasped and threw a hand over her eyes. I was buck naked. Standing in my full shriveled and wrinkled glory. Can I help it that I love to shock the ladies? When your day consists of a highly regimented set of endlessly repeating activities, you have to find ways to spice things up, right? You with me on this? Good.

"Oh my!" she said, her light brown skin flushing. She was a handsome woman and I guess more than my brain thought so. I looked down, pleased. It was working today! Must have been her perfume. Jasmine, I think?

"Morning, doc. What can I do for you?"

"Oh- I- " she turned and gathered up my bathrobe from the guest chair near my desk. Without looking back at me she held the robe between us like a shield. "Here you go."

"Thanks, doc. But I think I'll find something else to

wear," I said, and brushed passed her on my way to the closet.

"Very well, Richard, can you please meet me in my office after breakfast?"

"Love to!" I said. "Should I dress first?"

My best friend, Sheldon Majowski, is a big guy. And I mean that in every sense of the word. He's 6'4", tops 400 lb., and has a heart the size of a four-person re-entry capsule. He's also an off-the-charts genius. Big guy, see? He was a codebreaker in the 25th century. Quantum Entanglement Cryptanalysis was his thing.

Sheldon shuffled into to my room as Dr. Chopra ran off down the hall, still in a state of shock. Hey, they hired these people to watch over us and get inside our heads to make sure the containers weren't leaky. Problem was, half the time we were getting inside their heads. I mean, seriously, it's like locking up a bunch of alligators and putting baby gazelle in there to keep them in line. Sometimes I just have to shake my head.

"Breakfast is at 6:30am," Sheldon said seriously, as if he were confiding in me.

"S'up, Sheldon?"

"Don't want to be late."

"We won't be."

"Omelettes this morning. Can't miss omelet day."

I smiled at Sheldon. He was a good guy, but I wondered if he cracked more than codes back in the day. Though, that sneaky devil never lost a chess game. Omelettes and chess—a man has to have passions, right?

I limped down the hall after Sheldon. I know, it's the year 3478, why do I have a limp? Some damned neurological gremlin—causes joint pain too. Probably the same little bastard that caused my migraines. The explanation I got was too much exposure to cosmic rays. And the Rigel Mission engineers had said, "plenty of shielding. You'll be fine." Bald-faced liars!

As we strolled down the hall on our way to the cafeteria, we soaked in the scenery of ancient Britain's Cambridge University. We walked beside a river, on a grassy bank. Students at sculling practice glided atop the glassy water in long, thin boats. It was a warm spring morning, the smell of fresh cut grass in the air and a hint of some water flowers.

Of course we weren't actually seeing Cambridge, we were enjoying the daily wallpaper—a multi-sensory projection courtesy of our GNAT implants. I'd never been to Cambridge, so maybe this wasn't what it looked like at all 1,400 years ago. It was pleasant though.

"Boys," came a purr. It was Vihvee'N Soorehgaii, an old lady from Epsilon Eridani IV. Though, the Eridanii didn't age like we did. Vihvee'N looked to be in her 30's, but at heart, she was an Old Fart just like us. The Eridanii are humanoid, with silvery skin, black markings, and white hair, which was more like whisker-thin anemone—the stuff wriggled! And their sub-dermal musculature was akin to a snake, so they could climb trees like nobody's business. Though, at a glance, they had two legs, two arms, and Vihvee'N, well …she was well equipped up top. Hey, don't judge, I'm not dead yet!

"Morning, V," I said. She filed into line behind us as we grabbed our breakfast.

Sheldon blushed. He wasn't great around the ladies, and I'm pretty sure he had a thing for Vihvee'N. Unfortunately, she had a thing for me. At least I thought she did. Many of the Eridanii were highly empathic, some even telepaths. And I suspect Vihvee'N used her talents to play around with Sheldon and me on an emotional level. We didn't mind, we three were pals. It was all part of our daily game.

"What are you two handsome specimens of humanity up to on this fine morning?" she asked.

"Oh, you know, a little of this, a little of that," I said.

"Where's Hamid?" Vihvee'N asked. Hamid Farsoun was the fourth person in our little breakfast club.

I shrugged. "Had weird dreams last night. Said he was going to sleep in."

Vihvee'N stared at me, her head askew. "What did you do to Dr. Chopra this morning?"

I feigned ignorance. 'What ever do you mean?"

She rolled her eyes. "I felt her mind squawking clear across the quad. Must have been quite a show?"

I chuckled. Trays in hand, we found an empty table in the cafeteria, which the GNATs presented to us as some ancient piazza with little tables and umbrellas. Rome maybe?

"You should reserve such performances for a more *appreciative* audience." She reached out and caressed my mind

… could have been my leg, can't be sure. I was a bit fuzzy after she said that. Of course Sheldon was aghast at her flirtatious innuendo—though, I think he secretly enjoyed it.

"I'll have to make that right with Dr. Chopra. She wants to see me this morning after breakfast."

"In the dog house, eh? Want me to *smooth* things over?" she asked.

"No! Don't you dare! You'll get me mind-wiped."

"Dick's in trouble," Sheldon said.

"Isn't he always, Sheldon darling?" she said, and stroked his cheek with a hand which rippled and undulated sensuously.

Poor Sheldon, I thought he was going to wriggle out of his chair.

I knocked at Dr. Chopra's office door, currently an opaque glassteel.

"Come in," she said, and the door faded translucent. Dr. Chopra stood up from behind her desk.

"Good morning again, Richard."

"Morning, Dr. Chopra."

"Please, call me Calliope. May I call you Dick?"

"Oh, I really wish you would." I nodded.

She smiled. "Please, take a seat."

My legs shook as I tried to sit down, but I managed it. At least I didn't have a migraine this morning. You have to celebrate these little wins at my age. No migraine? That's a great day.

"I wanted to circle back to discuss the little incident from group last week," she said.

Little incident was a very politic way of putting it. I'd smacked some guy in the mouth. Hey, he had it coming, but we'll get into that later, I'm sure.

"Right," I said. "Might have been one of those muscle spasms, Doc."

"Now, Dick, I wasn't born yesterday."

No, but I was born 1,400 years ago. What's your point, little girl? I didn't say. I shrugged. "Maybe I missed my morning meds?"

She gave me one of those looks— you know, the one you give a naughty puppy? Or an adorable child you know is lying to you? Yeah, that one.

I felt a migraine coming on. "Listen, Doc, I- "

A scream shattered the quiet. It had come from outside the office somewhere.

Dr. Chopra leaped up startled. She must have engaged her NIC, because she stood silent for a moment. Us residents didn't get the neurally integrated comms, so I had to wait to ask her what was going on.

Her face took on a look of horrified disbelief. I'd never seen that look on anyone here. A pretty mellow bunch here at the Sanctuary.

"What is it, Doc?"

"Would you mind terribly waiting here for a moment?"

I offered an open handed go-for-it gesture. "I'll be here." I didn't feel like jumping up anyway. My joints ached.

She dashed out in a tizzy. I sat there for a moment, twiddling my thumbs, scratching my nose, but I'm not very good at doing nothing. I used to be a man who did things—important things. I missed those day.

I sat up like a rusty hinge, slow and creaking. Dr. Chopra had left her terminal unlocked. Hmm, couldn't hurt to take a peek. I eased into her chair. Now, my knees, hips and ass might be sore and slow, but my hands are like lightning. In under thirty-seconds I'd pried a panel from her terminal, shorted the security circuits and encoded my DNA to unlock her comms buffer. Child's play.

With a thumb on the biological interface, chemicals passed through my skin and fed the data directly to my brain.

—————————*Last message*—————————

ALERT: Resident Death

CIRCUMSTANCES: Unknown

LOCATION: ReRo3209

Shit! ReRo3209 meant Resident's Room 3209. That was my friend Hamid's. He was one of the few people from my own 21st century here, and one of the only I had anything in common with. Circumstances Unknown? That was bullshit. Every conceivable biometric parameter was monitored in here. The Garvey Neural Alpha-Wave Transceiver implants made sure of that.

At that moment I stopped being a resident.

Dick Wilson the operative had been reactivated.

I hobbled over to the porter and crawled onto the pad,

wincing at the various spurts of pain. "Resident's room 3209," I said. With no discernible motion or disturbance I was teleported to Hamid's floor.

I caught the scent of Dr. Chopra's Jasmine perfume from down the hall and felt a familiar stirring. Down boy!

The Doc had a pained look on her face and two guards were bent over Hamid's body. I noticed a line of blood had trickled from his nose and stained his white mustache.

"What happened?" I asked.

Dr. Chopra turned back to look at me. "Richard, you shouldn't be here."

"But I am. Jesus, I just talked with him this morning. What happened? "

"We're not sure."

"How can you *not* be sure? I thought your projected cessations were extremely accurate?"

She nodded. "It is. We calculate it starting at childhood and it's updated for a person's entire life. Usually we have the PC calculated to within minutes of actual death, but it's still just a highly educated guess." She gave my a sympathetic shrug. "I read in your file that you two were friends. I'm sorry. He was a contemporary?"

I nodded. "Yeah. A couple of decades apart, but close enough so we could talk football and movies. Let me know what you find out, ok?"

"Of course. Let's re-schedule our session for tomorrow?"

I nodded and walked away. I was going to miss that old fart.

MONDAY, APRIL 8TH, 3478

THE NEXT MORNING I WAS distracted during my chess game with Sheldon. He could tell, but didn't bitch about it. Even Sheldon had bags under his eyes. I guess we were all still feeling Hamid's death.

"You look like crap, Sheldon."

"Bad dreams," he said.

"I can imagine. I didn't sleep well either."

"Sorry about Hamid," he said.

"Thanks."

"You could teach me about football. Then we could talk

about it."

I laughed and Sheldon smiled, nodding enthusiastically. "Maybe I will."

Sheldon picked up his rook to take my pawn and stopped suddenly. His eyes rolled back in his head and his face cratered into the table. His heavy jowls scattered the chess pieces and toppled the board.

"Sheldon! Nurse!"

As I watched the orderlies taking Sheldon's body away on a contragrav gurney, Vihvee'N held my arm, radiating an aura of soothing emotions. Even that didn't quench my sorrow. This was another unexplained death. The Sanctuary has a projected cessation for each and every resident. The day before your PC they let you know, so you could say your goodbyes and get ready. Much less disruptive that way. People dropping dead in their rooms or on chessboards was just bullshit. Sanctuary, my ass.

"Dick, you know it's only an estimate," Vihvee'N said, clearly picking up my surface thoughts.

"V, in the five years I've been here, they've never been off this much. Then to have it happen twice in two days?

Once is chance, twice is coincidence. If it happens a third time, it's a pattern."

"Poor thing. We'll get through it together." She laid her head on my shoulder.

My chess partner was dead. That really kicked my day sideways. I mean, Sheldon was a great partner. Who else is going to play with me? Vivian claims she can play, but I think it's all pretense so she can get me into bed. Who can blame her, I'm a ruggedly handsome guy—by rugged I mean wrinkled, worn and ready to be discarded.

Though, I was glad Vihvee'N was here. She was my last friend. If anything happened to her I would lose my shit.

Monday, April 8th, 3478

THE NEXT MORNING I WAS distracted during my chess game with Sheldon. He could tell, but didn't bitch about it. Even Sheldon had bags under his eyes. I guess we were all still feeling Hamid's death.

"You look like crap, Sheldon."

"Bad dreams," he said.

"I can imagine. I didn't sleep well either."

"Sorry about Hamid," he said.

"Thanks."

"You could teach me about football. Then we could talk about it."

I laughed and Sheldon smiled, nodding enthusiastically.

"Maybe I will."

Sheldon picked up his rook to take my pawn and stopped suddenly. His eyes rolled back in his head and his face cratered into the table. His heavy jowls scattered the chess pieces and toppled the board.

"Sheldon! Nurse!"

As I watched the orderlies taking Sheldon's body away on a contragrav gurney, Vihvee'N held my arm, radiating an aura of soothing emotions. Even that didn't quench my sorrow. This was another unexplained death. The Sanctuary has a projected cessation for each and every resident. The day before your PC they let you know, so you could say your goodbyes and get ready. Much less disruptive that way. People dropping dead in their rooms or on chessboards was just bullshit. Sanctuary, my ass.

"Dick, you know it's only an estimate," Vihvee'N said,

clearly picking up my surface thoughts.

"V, in the five years I've been here, they've never been off this much. Then to have it happen twice in two days? Once is chance, twice is coincidence. If it happens a third time, it's a pattern."

"Poor thing. We'll get through it together." She laid her head on my shoulder.

My chess partner was dead. That really kicked my day sideways. I mean, Sheldon was a great partner. Who else is going to play with me? Vivian claims she can play, but I think it's all pretense so she can get me into bed. Who can blame her, I'm a ruggedly handsome guy—by rugged I mean wrinkled, worn and ready to be discarded.

Though, I was glad Vihvee'N was here. She was my last friend. If anything happened to her I would lose my shit.

Tuesday, April 9th, 3478

I STEPPED OUT OF MY room to head for breakfast. Sheldon's absence was conspicuous. He'd met me for hundreds of mornings. Vihvee'N and Hamid lived on the other side of the quad, so they usually walked together and we all met up at the cafeteria for breakfast.

This morning Vihvee'N had walked to my side of the building first and caught up to me five meters down the hall —or rather, some cobblestone street in the Left Bank of Paris in the 19th century—today's wallpaper. She took my hand and gave it a squeeze.

"I need coffee bad."

"Why don't you just let them implant a caffeine gland?"

"Because, I like coffee. Plus, they already mess with my innards too much."

"Are you handling Hamid and Sheldon's death?" Vihvee'N asked.

"Handling, yes. Handling well, no." We kept walking and I caught whiff of freshly baked french bread. Damn that was amazing wallpaper. "Let me ask you a question, V. If your people don't age externally, how do you know you're old?"

Vihvee'N grinned at me. "Eridanii feel old age, just as you do. Your joints ache, your eyesight fades. Our control over emotions and intellectual faculties fade. I feel it every bit as acutely as you do your sore knee."

"So that explains the flirting?"

She shook her head. "No. I just enjoy doing that," she said deadpan. Then mentally pushed a very graphic image of me and her … well, never mind. You get the picture. She giggled. Still a girl at heart.

After breakfast I went to neural therapy. It was supposed to help with the migraines and the achy joints caused by whatever the heck was wrong with me. I had been cautiously optimistic, but after three weeks I'd seen no real improvement. Each session they stuffed me into this neural-therapy machine; it was the hideous offspring of an old-school MRI and torpedo tube.

The inner collar of the tube glowed and pulsed. My body jerked while my brain itched. I was running through a mental inventory of any clues from the scenes of Hamid's and Sheldon's deaths. One of the things I used to do for STD, was find causal patterns—sort of like social multivariate analysis.

While left brained guys like Sheldon were almost human computers; born with brains that had massive processing power and memory. My gift was neither right brained nor left brained, but one that seemed to straddle the hemispheres perfectly. I was able to synthesize and analyze that beautiful symphony of art and science. I had a knack for making bold leaps and linking unrelated facts and impressions. Which was why I was such a good operator— among other reasons.

As I lied there twitching and jerking, trying to concentrate, a burst of multi-sensory input rocked my psyche.

I stood under two blazing suns; one yellow, one blue. An endless sea of white sand stretched out in front of me. I was very disoriented. I wore a suit of some kind—a vacc-suit? Maybe powered armor? I queried the HUD projected on my visor. Chronograph read 02:09:43 1/19/2812. What the fuck? I had never been to 2812—ever! Nor was I allowed to. My STD indoctrination date was 2936. We were forbidden from traveling to a time before our indoc. That was the only capital crime in known space-time. The only thing that would get you erased.

My body started moving, but I didn't do it. I tried to stop my feet, move my arms—nothing. It was like watching a qvid, but much more intense. Qvids engaged all five senses, but this was somehow more real.

The images started to accelerate, like someone hit fast-forward. My brain told me I wanted to vomit, but the *me* who was moving kept on trucking. In a flash I was over a dune. I saw a single story building. A shuttle rested on a silcrete pad on the far side.

Two men in scout-suits erupted from the building. I began firing a plasma rifle which I'd been holding. They went down, smoking holes through their armor and bodies where the plasma had bored through them like a laser-drill.

The next set of images sped up so fast I couldn't make sense of them, but I exited the other side of the building at a run. An explosion lit up the sky around me and knocked me to the ground. I landed face first in the white sand. Then I saw the cockpit of the shuttle and the images began to fade.

Suddenly I was falling! I looked down at my feet and spied a building roof rising up to meet me. I must have been in a contragrav harness because I was falling straight and decelerating. I landed on the rooftop with a thump. I caught sight of a moon low in the blue sky—Luna. I was on Earth. The same sort of sequence repeated twice more: I killed people, set of a powerful charge, and escaped. The last trip was to a planet I recognized as Eridani III—I'd been there during a mission decades ago.

Finally the strange visions were replaced by the tube of

the neural-therapy machine. "What the hell just happened?" I demanded.

"What do you mean, Mr. Wilson?" asked the tech.

"My brain just went haywire. Did you zap me or something?"

"No, sir. I did warn you that twitching and muscle spams were a common side-effect of the treatment."

"This was nothing like that."

"I'll pull you out and run a full diagnostic on the machine, sir. I apologize for any discomfort."
"You went where?" Vihvee'N asked.

"I don't know exactly. The first place was a vast desert on a planet orbiting a yellow and blue star stars. The *where* isn't as important as the *when*. The first trip was to 2812! That's 124 years before my indoc."

Vihvee'N's eyes went wide. "Oh."

"Yeah, oh!"

"Were they memories?"

"Sort of. Now they feel like memories, but while I lie in that tube, I could swear I was also on those three planets. Though I wasn't in control of my body."

"Perhaps the neural therapy stimulated old memories? You are getting older, love. You may have just forgotten about those missions."

"No God damned way, V. I might be a bit slower picking out my favorite foods on the menu, but I remember every single op I ever ran."

"Then what do you think it was?"

I shook my head. "Dunno." Then it struck me … "Dreams …"

"Pretty vivid dreams," Vihvee'N offered.

"No, not mine. Both Hamid and Sheldon mentioned dreams before they died."

A look of concern followed by a wave of wrenching emotions emanated from Vihvee'N. They hit me like a bucket of cold water and she saw the look of shock on my face.

"Sorry, Dick. I didn't mean to do that. See, I am getting old."

I pushed my chair out from the table. "I need to get to the freezer. Now! Otherwise I'll be dead."

We hobbled down a long corridor toward the intake room,

which we liked to call the freezer. It was instantiated in a bubble outside space-time, and was used to fine tune new resident's temporal destination before they arrived.

Vihvee'N had to slow down so I could keep up—God damned joint pain! "Can you confuse the guard a little? You know, with your Eridanii tricks?"

She grinned at me. "My Eridanii *tricks*?"

"You know what I mean. Don't split hairs."

"It's called telepathy, Dick. And yes I will use my *Eridanii tricks* on the guard. But then what?"

"Leave that to me. And hey, I've always wondered, if you're a true telepath and not just an empath, why didn't they put you in the Restricted Wing?"

"Like you, Colonel, much of my dossier is classified. Including the full extent of my *Eridanii tricks*." She winked at me.

"How the hell do you know my rank?" I was truly shocked because my background was a very closely guarded secret. Dick Wilson wasn't even my real name. In fact, I don't even know what it was anymore—they wiped it when I joined the black ops division of STD.

She just smiled as we came into view of two guards flanking the door to the freezer. "Good afternoon, gentlemen," she said. Both of them grinned like pubescent boys at their first woman. Damn, did she work it. Her sub-dermal layers of Eridanii muscle rippling, causing her curves to undulate in a fashion that bellydancers would kill to learn.

While they enjoyed their show, I slipped in behind them and applied a firm karate chop to their subclavian arteries, rendering them unconscious. It was kind of like the Vulcan neck pinch—and yes, that shit actually worked.

"Ooh, I like a dangerous man." She purred at me.

It took both of us to drag each of the guards into the freezer. I remember a day when I could have carried both of them over my shoulders—at the same time. Getting old sucks.

I shut the door and disabled the panel on the exterior so nobody could disturb us; at least not for a while. Vihvee'N tapped the control console on the wall and a blue light suffused the room—hence the name, the freezer. We now existed in a pocket outside of time.

"Are you going to tell me why we're here?" she asked.

I nodded "Because … despite my bitching and complaining, I still enjoy life. And I'd like to see if you can actually play chess."

She gave me a small smile and stroked my cheek. "What's going on?"

"I told you yesterday; once is chance, twice is coincidence, three times and it's a pattern. Both Hamid and Sheldon complained of odd dreams just hours before they died. Then I have these strange memories or experiences? Dreams?"

She nodded grimly, understanding my meaning.

"We have a serial killer on the loose. Either an individual, a government agency, or some foreign power. I don't know which—yet. These were no God damned accidents!"
"You're sure this will work?" Vihvee'N asked.

"No. I'm not." I said. I was pulling crystals out of a blank security panel in the wall and re-routing various control functions. "But I'm not one to just lay down and die, V." The panel lit up and I could navigate the interface.

"What are you looking for?"

"Evidence."

"Of what?"

"I don't know exactly, but I will once I see it." I'd hacked into the residents record files. Our GNAT implants performed a number of functions: they were biometric monitors and transceivers; they allowed us to experience the multi-sensory wallpaper by manipulating the alpha waves in our brains; and they uploaded most of our thoughts and memories to the central computer core. I know, that sounds very big-brother. Trust me, it would never have flown in my 21st century, but we waved such trivial rights like personal freedom on joining the STD program. The missions we undertook and the things we knew, had to be contained and preserved.

In theory, the memory files of the central computer core were inaccessible to anyone except under direct order of the Secretary of Space-Time Defense. Those records were stored in case of dire emergency. In practice, sneaky bastards like me could hack any system—that's the kind of thing we were trained to do, after all.

I started by reviewing Hamid's memories the night before he died. All the usual crap showed up—rem sleep black screen, and then … a memory of a dream. Three dreams. I double checked and these dreams correlated to fragmented memories. I pulled up the first.

"Holy shit," I whispered.

"What?" Vihvee'N asked.

I held up a finger as I scanned through the other two dreams to be sure. Yep, they were the same as mine. Three planets, three missions. I dove into Sheldon's file next. Same thing.

I turned to Vihvee'N. "Someone's been screwing around with our time-stream. I need to do one thing before I explain." I turned back to the control panel and hacked my own files. I wasn't interested in memories, I could recall them at will. I was interested in deactivating my GNAT and freezing my profile. Done. Now hopefully I would live—if only for a while longer.

I slumped down to the floor, wincing as various jolts of pain shot through my limbs and as I finally recognized the migraine blossoming in my head. Vihvee'N sat beside me and rubbed my temples.

"Someone is deliberately altering our time-stream.

Hamid, then Sheldon, and now me, were recruited for three missions in our pasts. Though they're missions I'm only now remembering?"

"What? Is that possible?"

"Of course it's possible. We have time travel technology. We *can* do almost anything. Usually the STD keeps a good handle on things, but now, someone is running amok. They recruited at least three of us retirees in our pasts for some mission they wanted off the books. That means that at a minimum, they travelled back into our timelines."

"Two things," Vihvee'N said, "is it possible you did the mission but the erased the memory of it? That's pretty common in black ops. Second, why recruit retirees?"

"Yes to the first question, but when the STD erases a memory, there is no way to recall it. It's not like they mask it, they physically remove the engrams from your brain. Second, because the authorities in our timeline wouldn't notice new memories in retirees. They're locked down in the core. Unless there was some huge emergency, or an investigation, nobody would ever have seen them. And if the retiree suddenly wanted to talk about those new memories—kill them. As they did to Hamid and Sheldon."

"How?" she asked.

"They inserted a manufacturing flaw into their GNAT implants. I suspect mine's been altered as well, or would have been shortly. That's why I needed to get to the freezer and deactivate my GNAT."

"Two more questions: first, how can what they do to the GNATs in the past affect you now? I thought the Sanctuary was a protected timeline? Second, why you three?"

"They must have someone on the inside—probably one of the maintenance engineers—someone able to hack the freezer and allow a stream of new events into our protected timeline. And why us three? Skill-sets, I suppose. Hamid was a security consultant, Sheldon was cryptanalyst, and I was … well, am, a guy who does the other things." She took my meaning. Hell, she probably read my surface thoughts. I wasn't ashamed of what I'd done—it was all in the service of maintaining a stable society, after all. But I had some pretty ugly memories. Memories which I'd just as soon forget.

"We were tapped to infiltrate and destroy three top-secret installations," I continued. "On Earth, Eridani III, and some other planet in a binary star system." I anticipated her next question. "I don't know what they have in common, yet. First I need to identify the first planet. Then maybe I can start making some correlations."

I got seventeen minutes to scour the data-core before the security panel indicated that someone was hacking back into the freezer controls. "Shit. They found us." I tried to lock them out, but it was no use.

Suddenly Vihvee'N slammed her head into the hard wall, gashing open her forehead, blood flowing down her face.

"What the hell?" I said.

The door to the freezer slid open and four guards in armor and carrying heavy stun weapons closed in on us.

"Help me!" Vihvee'N screamed. "He's gone mad!"

I just gaped at her. That traitorous old bitch! Was she in on it? I surrendered without a fight. I was too old to take on four guards. I might still be able to manage one on my own, but four? Screw that. If today was my day, then so be it. My friends were dead, and the last one had betrayed me. What's the point of living. I shook my head at Vihvee'N as they dragged me away. Why? I mouthed. A medic was tending to her wound. She broke eye contact and turned away from me. I lay in my room, which was now a cell, the door locked from the outside; alone with my thoughts. Two friends dead, one a turncoat. So far this was shaping up to be a shitty week of epic proportions. Had they got to her? Whoever the hell *they* were? I needed to focus. I had to stop running over these negative patterns in an endless feedback loop.

Remember your training recruit, and you just might live through this, a drill instructor had said. I began breathing methodically, centering my mind—which, let me tell you, gets much harder as you near the edge of the old age cliff.

Parsing through the new memories I began to correlate data points. What did Earth and Eridani III have in common? Well, that would be worth the risk of erasure, or causing a war. That certainly trimmed the list down. Anyone traveling before their indoc date would have to be insane— which I was not—or be ordered to do so. But why?

I started with memories of the operation to Earth. I searched for clues in the terrain around the facility, inside the laboratory, anywhere. I noted a name tag on one of the scientists—Planck. I'd killed him. I'd killed everyone in the lab. Why did the name Planck ring a bell? Holy shit! Max Planck was the man who originated quantum theory. Karl Planck, his great-grandson many times removed, was the guy who experimentally proved temporal mechanics.

My heart was pounding now. I tried to maintain some balance so I could continue to analyze the situation. I jumped to memories of Eridani III.

The Eridanii lab rats didn't wear name-tags, but I recognized the face of Lorkir Ors'Adai. You guess it. He also pioneered temporal mechanics. That made deducing the name of the first planet easy—Rigel VII. Three scientists cracked time travel at about the same time. And apparently … I'd killed them all.

But hold on a second … if I killed all the people who invented time travel, wouldn't that mean the Sanctuary should no longer exist?

That evening, just after supper, the door to my room chimed and Dr. Chopra walked in, a sad look on her face.

I sat up on my bed. "Hey Doc."

"How are faring, Mr. Wilson?"

Mr. Wilson? What happened to at least calling me Richard? Now even the Doc had turned against me? "Oh, you know … hanging in there."

"Why did you do it?"

"Do what?"

"Kill them?"

How did she know about those ops? I sighed. What did it really matter? "I don't know why I did it. I must have been ordered to."

She looked aghast. "By whom?"

"I can't remember." I couldn't.

"They were your friends, Richard," she said pleading.

What? "My friends?"

"Hamid and Sheldon. You considered them friends, did you not?"

"I did *not* kill them!" What the fuck was going on now? "Why would you even say that?"

She shook her head at me like I'd disappointed her. My mother used to do that. I hated it. "Richard, you know in cases of emergency, such as investigating murder, we are allowed access to the computer core records. They had memories of you just before they died."

You have to be shitting me. Someone was really screwing me over. I never liked being screwed over. In fact I was famous for payback. That deterred would-be over-screwers. Game on.

Now, how was a broken-down, former operator supposed to escape his retirement home? These were situations not covered in training, I assure you.

Wednesday, April 10th, 3478

THE NEXT MORNING A GUARD delivered my breakfast. I had a lump in my throat. I'd been here for almost five years, and every day I'd walked to the cafeteria. Remember, I like routine.

As the guard made to leave, Vihvee'N appeared, smiling at the guard who stared blankly at her for a moment. Vihvee'N slipped into my room and the guard left with saying another word.

Was she here to kill me? She was like a sister to me. Ok,

maybe not a sister—a kissing cousin?

She smiled at me. At least I'd die looking at a beautiful woman. Worse ways to go—I should know.

"Just kill me quick."

She laughed. "But you haven't taught me to play chess yet?"

"What?"

She closed here eyes and I felt a torrent of emotion and sensations flood my mind. She shared her plan with me.

"An act?" I said.

"I knew they'd lock you up. If we were both incarcerated, then I couldn't break you out? Now could I?"

"You crafty old bitch!"

"Shall I take that as a compliment?"

"You may indeed."

"Now, what's your plan, Colonel?"

Vihvee'N had quite a repertoire of mental magic. Tapping into the GNAT with her mind, she could project her own wallpaper, in effect, disguising us from the guards and other onlookers.

"We need to find a temporal engineer," I said.

"Restricted Wing?"

I nodded.

"I can get us in."

"You're a handy lady to have around, V."

"So they used to tell me."

The restricted wing housed residents that need very close monitoring; people like Vihvee'N, though she'd somehow evaded that restricted designation. They also housed retired temporal engineers—didn't want rogue assets messing with the time stream, now did they? Clearly they'd missed someone. And it had to be a retiree—active STD assets were the most closely monitored sentient creatures in known space-time. Retirees, however, were not. Which is why they'd gone back in time and recruited us before retirement—after our time-streams were effectively frozen and no longer being monitored. Don't ask me how all that shit works, I'm no engineer.

Two heavily armed guards flanked the door into the Restricted Wing. Due to Vihvee'N's projection, or to her Eridanii tricks, they remained ignorant of our presence as she *convinced* them to open the door.

I glanced over at Vihvee'N with a look of wonder.

She gave me a cute shrug.

The Restricted Wing had a different feel to it. Of course I was seeing it sans wallpaper. Even our own wing was normally experienced as some interesting place from another time. Undecorated, as it were, it was like any retirement home or hospital—sterile, boring, and sure to drive you mad. Thank God for multi-sensory wallpaper. The Restricted Wing was more prison like. It had a darker, more ominous feel to it.

"I need to access the patient roster here," I said, "to see if there's anyone that can help."

We approached a nurse standing with her hand on the access pad of a terminal. Vihvee'N touched her shoulder and the woman began mentally calling up a resident roster on the screen.

"Have her search for temporal engineers," I said.

Vihvee'N nodded and one name appeared on the screen. She grinned.

A seemingly middle-aged Eridanii man sat on his bed with a Qreader. He looked up and gaped.

"My Lady!" he scrambled off his bed and knelt to Vihvee'N. "What an honor!"

"Are you messing with his head?" I asked.

She let out a small laugh. "No. Dick, allow me to introduce, Vaxt Zhanliren, Eridani IV's most accomplished temporal engineer during my term of service."

I nodded, he nodded back.

"My Lady, if I may ask, why are you here?" Vaxt asked.

"We need your help," she said.

"Anything for the Silver Widow," he said bowing.

Yeah, there was a story there. I was sure of that. But we had more pressing issues to attend to—like saving our space-time continuum.

I explained our situation to Vaxt.

"This is not the work of an individual," he concluded. "This has to be a coup by some faction."

"What about outside forces?" I asked. "A species or culture we've not encountered yet?"

"Possible, I suppose," Vaxt said.

"And the big gorilla in the room? If I killed all the inventors of time travel, why the hell isn't the Sanctuary gone? Shouldn't this whole branch of the timeline be null and void?"

Vaxt shook his head. "No. That's one of the reasons the Sanctuary was built as it was. It's designed to protect retirees from changes to their own timelines. For all I know, time outside this facility has been irrevocably reset, re-vectored. In here though, we're quite safe."

"But how do we fix it? If we're stuck in a place with no tech to facilitate time travel, then what?" I asked. "I can't just live out my days here knowing what I've done. And worse, not knowing who pulled the strings."

"Not to worry, Mr. Wilson. Of course we have tech to time travel. The very nature of this facility is built on that tech."

"Explain," I asked.

"The Sanctuary is not one place—it is many places—across time. Think about it. How many people do you think reside in this facility?"

I shrugged. "Ten-thousand, maybe?"

"A good estimate," Vaxt said. "Now, across centuries and many worlds, imagine all the people who have worked for

Space-Time Defense …" He let that hang.

I nodded. "Yeah. I guess you're right. Why did that never occur to me?"

He laughed. "GNATs."

"What do you mean?" I asked.

"The GNATs provide biometric data, the wallpaper, and, they provide a neural feedback loop networked through all the residents. The designers augment that feedback with certain thoughts, or in some cases, block certain thoughts."

"Mind control?" I asked.

"Essentially, yes. But it's subtle. So subtle you didn't even notice. It never occurred to you that ten-thousand retirees in centuries of the STD's history was a low number."

"Rat bastards! So how many are there?"

He threw up his hands. "I don't know. Far more than ten-thousand. If you get me to the temporal reactor, then I may be able to help."

"Temporal reactor?" I asked.

"It powers the Sanctuary. It incorporates the functions of a standard power rector and includes a temporal multiplexor. That multiplexor generates various instances of the Sanctuary. Think of them like virtual computer environments. But these environments are entirely real, at least to whomever is inside them. There could be thousands of Sanctuaries in existence. Millions perhaps."

We began making our way through the Restricted Wing, heading toward the Temporal Reactor room. Vihvee'N had included Vaxt in the illusion she projected to the other residents and we had no trouble. Until we did.

Vihvee'N gasped. She bent over at the waist and grabbed her head.

"V, you ok?" I asked.

Vaxt put a hand on her shoulder.

Suddenly residents started noticing us. "Shit," I mumbled. "C'mmon, V." I grabbed one arm and Vaxt grabbed the other. We dragged her toward the exit.

She screamed and her head lolled down. I noticed blood seeping from her nose.

"V," I whispered.

We lay her down and I checked for a pulse. Nothing. They'd killed her. All because she'd helped me. Vaxt was stunned. All I could think about was—why hadn't I disabled her GNAT when I disabled mine? Why? Because I'm a selfish old prick and was focused on me.

A guard approached us, carrying a heavy stun-rifle. I made no offensive moves, feigning sorrow, sobbing over Vihvee'N. I *was* sad, but I put that shit in a little jar. I'd open it later.

He bent over to grab my arm and I kicked out at his ankle, knocking him off balance and causing him to fall face first next to me. I slammed an elbow down onto the back of his skull, knocking him senseless. I picked up his stun-rifle. Time for payback.

I grabbed Vaxt, and winced at the pain in my elbow. "Get on your feet, Vaxt. We've got work to do."
Getting around was made much more difficult now that Vihvee'N was gone. We had no mental camouflage and the guards knew where I was. But did they know where I was headed?

I reduced the setting on the stun-rifle so that I wouldn't completely incapacitate the next guard. I needed some help. The guard who rounded a corner got a mild stun, sending him to his knees. That's all the help I needed.

I manipulated two nerve clusters until he screamed for me to kill him. "Do I have your attention now?"

"Yes!" he said panting.

"You will open the door to the temporal reactor. Do you understand me?"

He hesitated for a moment, so I tweaked the nerve clusters, causing him to howl. "Yes!"

The guard opened the door. I nodded, dialed up the stun setting and sent him to sleep with a quick shot. I motioned for Vaxt to enter and followed him in.

I was not prepared for what I saw. I'd seen fusion reactors, even anti-matter reactors. This contraption looked nothing like any rector I'd seen or even imagined.

Firstly, the room was as cold as a meat freezer. I could see the first breath I exhaled. It seemed to crystalize and fall before my eyes. The shape of the room was like an old lightbulb, with the bulge maybe 100 meters in diameter. The central feature being a hovering sphere of black liquid. At least that's how I saw it. It seemed to be spinning on one axis, as if caught in a quantum levitation field. Around the perimeter of the bulge, thousands of high-energy laser beams converged on the black sphere. The beams formed a glowing, purple spider web around the sphere. Eerie!

"Over here," Vaxt said.

He stood at the end of the neck of the lightbulb, just before the bulge, at a control panel of sorts.

"What do you want me to do?" Vaxt asked.

"What can you do?"

"I can manipulate the multiplexor and send you anywhere and anywhen you like. Perhaps you can escape."

"No. I need to fix this."

"I'm not sure you can, Mr. Wilson. Think of all the variables. Where would you even begin?"

"The GNATs," I said.

"What about them?"

"Someone introduced a manufacturing flaw into Hamid and Sheldon's GNATs. Mine too, likely. I was able to disable mine before it killed me. Is there a way I can travel somewhere, then get back here without access to a temporal-transporter?"

"I think so. Yes."

Vaxt rigged up a sort of homing beacon that would reset my

temporal resonance and return me to the Sanctuary— essentially it was an emergency temporal transporter. It was crude, but he didn't have time for anything fancier.

I examined the device that looked like a huge wristwatch with prominent central button.

"You can only use it once," Vaxt said. "And no, I can't make another. Also, it will have to transport you to a point in time earlier than our present. The time-stream for our present is too strong. And … as soon as I transport you out of here the authorities will be alerted."

"Does that mean you'll- "

"Be arrested? Yes. Then erased."

"Shit."

"It doesn't matter, Mr. Wilson. If someone is trying to manipulate our time streams, then it's likely I won't be alive long enough to erase. Or for that matter, perhaps the temporal authorities no longer exist?"

That was a disturbing thought. "Call me, Dick."

Vaxt nodded. "Ready, Dick?"

"As I'll ever be." I knew the GNATs were made to order for each resident, a day before retirement and their trip to the Sanctuary. And there was only one factory that produced them. The upshot was that our target was small. The downside was that it might not even exist anymore. I could be porting into oblivion. But if I couldn't fix this, what did it matter?

"Hey, Vaxt. One question before you send me into potential oblivion. Why did you call Vihvee'N Lady?"

"Because she is. Do you understand how the Eridani IV ruling class is chosen?"

"Of course," I said, "they're chosen based on their empathic skills. The stronger the empath, the better they understand their people, and the better they rule."

"Just so," Vaxt said.

"Then what was Vihvee'N doing here at the Sanctuary? If she's a member of the ruling class, shouldn't she live at the palace?"

"She made a great sacrifice for our people, Dick. Few people know the story. As a temporal engineer I had access to the most sensitive information, so I knew of her. She was indeed a powerful empath, but she was also an even more powerful telepath. She gave up her position in the ruling family to serve the Space-Time Defense program. Her fame grew, and legend blossomed. Few knew who she really was, but stories were shared about an Eridanii woman called the Silver Widow—a play on the Earth's black widow spider."

"Well, holy shit." What else could I say. She and I had a lot of catching up to do—assuming I got all this mess fixed. A man has to dream, no? I nodded for Vaxt to send me on my way.

Time travel is strange. Something I never got used to. It feels like you're being electrocuted by ice. Make sense? No? Well neither does time travel to a grunt like me. Trust me, it feels nasty. As my body went numb and my limbs froze, my vision went dark.

I woke up shivering on a factory floor, the stun rifle beside me. Jesus, I was cold! My teeth chattered like an old chainsaw. But that was a good thing. It meant I was alive. And it meant that time travel was still possible outside the Sanctuary.

I rubbed my shoulders frantically, trying to massage life back into them.

Once I felt like my body temp was on an upward

trajectory, I retrieved the stun rifle and ratcheted down the setting to mild stun. Then I hid and waited. A bright screen on the wall scrolled the message "52 minutes util first shift". Good, I wouldn't have to wait too long.

I must have nodded off, because I jerked up at the sound of an indicator bell. First shift had started. I stayed hidden behind some crates. To be honest, I wasn't sure what I was looking for … that is, until I saw her.

Vihvee'N? If it wasn't her, it was a damned good clone. She was dressed like the other factory workers who were streaming in, clad in white coveralls. I knew it was her because of her facial markings. The black markings on an Eridanii were as individual as fingerprints, and I'd known Vihvee'N for over two years now. I saw that face every morning. She must have been projecting some kind of illusion, because the other workers seemed oblivious to her nosing around their workstations. Didn't even bat an eye when she borrowed tools, moved boxes, whatever. She was so much more than an empath. She was the Silver Widow. She was Vihvee'N Soorehgaii. She was my friend. And she was up to something.

I walked toward her casually, but the factory workers didn't like the look of me and their whispering got Vihvee'N's attention.

I called out to her. "Vihvee'N Soorehgaii!"

Her head whipped around like a viper, her eyes narrowing. I recognized that look. Not from my friend Vihvee'N, but from an enemy about to try to kill me. I'd seen it many times. Before she had a chance to mess with my head, I fired the stun-rifle.

She convulsed and fell to the factory floor, the workers now panicked and scattering.

I stood over her. "Vihvee'N, why?"

Still twitching from the stun, her face was a mix of agony and confusion. "How do you know my name?"

"What do you mean? You're Vihvee'N Soorehgaii. My friend." I could see the pain fading in her expression and her body relaxing.

"Friend?" she asked.

"Dick Wilson. You don't remember me?" What the hell had they done to her? I felt a strong wave sympathy and good will toward her. My friend, Vihvee'N. I pulled the trigger again, stunning her for a second time. "Oh no you don't! I've had my head messed with enough lately."

Was that it? Was it over? All I had to do was take her back and the timeline would be reset. The doctors at the Sanctuary could reset Vihvee'N's brain. Surely whatever programming or mind alterations they'd done to her could be reversed? But then who sent her? If I reset this timeline, wouldn't *they* just send someone else?

As I ran through all these permutations I felt a tingly, icy feeling creeping through my limbs. I fell to my knees, freezing.

I woke up in an enormous control room. Something far larger than the temporal reactor room in the Sanctuary. Men in STD uniforms lined the walls. Some manning stations, others milling about.

An older man with two stars on his uniform approached me as I stood up—a general. "Welcome back, Colonel."

"Excuse me?"

He nodded patiently. "You're gonna feel a bit confused for a few hours. That's normal."

"Normal for what? I take it this is not the Sanctuary?"

"No, Dick. This is not the Sanctuary. Your mission was a complete success."

"What mission? Where's Vihvee'N Soorehgaii?"

A guy in a white lab coat—a doctor I assumed—began scanning me and taking readings as I continued talking to the general.

"She's been taken into custody, Dick."

"Will you be able to help her? Someone's altered her memories, or wiped her. I don't know. She's not acting like her old self."

"That's because she isn't her old self."

I said nothing, hoping he would elaborate.

"Dick, you've been in deep cover for over five years. We knew the Silver Widow ended up at the Sanctuary, but didn't know who she was, or her precise retirement date. We had a window of about 10 years. That was the boundary duration of your mission to find the assassin."

"What?" I suddenly realized that I had no migraine—not even a twinge. Nor did my joints feel sore. At all. I lifted a hand up and examined it. My skin … it was smooth!

The general grinned. "Body feel better? Back to your fit

forties."

"So my retirement ... *was* the mission?" I asked.

The general nodded.

"I remember five years there. Did that actually happen?"

"Uh huh. Sure did. We had to implant you with false memories to start. But yes, I'm sorry to say that your five years subjective is accurate."

"But, if Vihvee'N was the assassin, who killed her?"

"We terminated her in the Sanctuary using the same trick her colleagues employed on Hamid and Sheldon. And were going to do to you. But we still needed you to catch her in the future. Which, you did. Well done, by the way. She's the most elusive agent we've been up against. We failed this very mission six times, altering variables with each iteration. Lucky number seven was the charm it seems."

I'd tuned him out at that point. "My friends ..." I muttered. Hamid, Sheldon ...Vihvee'N. My mind drifted for a moment as I internalized the loss. I was happy there. God, I needed a cup of coffee—no migraine this time, just a burning desire for french roast. I noticed the device on my wrist. I smiled. "Screw it," I said, slapping the button on my homing beacon.

`

Tuesday, June 27th, 3476

TWO YEARS EARLIER - TUESDAY, JUNE 27th, 3476

Hamid, Sheldon and me sat in the cafeteria having breakfast, as we'd done for years now. It was a little ritual, a routine. And at my age, routine is good.

"Any new Qvids in the library?" Hamid asked.

"Nothing worth watching," I said.

"Good omelette," Sheldon said.

Yeah, he really liked his omelets.

"Oy," Hamid said, elbowing me. "New fish—3 o'clock"

I spied an Eridanii woman. Damn they looked good for

old folks. They didn't age much on the outside, not like we humans did. This old lady looked to be in her mid-thirties. And boy, was she stacked! And boy, was she observant. I was *so* busted. She caught me checking her out and grinned, vectoring over to our table.

"Morning boys. Mind if I sit here?"

Sheldon shook his head, stunned by the Eridanii woman's beauty. He was a smart man, but not so good with the ladies.

"My name's Vihvee'N, but you all can call me V. I have a feeling we're going to be fast friends."

I nodded, smiling, because I already knew we would be.

Also by Hugh B. Long

Abhuman

Of Ice & Magic

The Yggdrasil Codex: Book 0

Star Wolves - The Tribes of Yggdrasil: Book 1

Star Fury - The Tribes of Yggdrasil: Book 2

Star Viking - The Tribes of Yggdrasil: Book 3

Want more free books and stories?

Signup for my new releases updates, and you can download more free stories!

Go to this link to subscribe: http://goo.gl/zYa6IF

Like Norse Mythology & Viking Culture?

Check out my non-fiction books written as Eoghan Odinsson:

Northern Lore - A Field Guide to the Northern Mind, Body, and Spirit

Northern Wisdom: The Havamal, Tao of the Vikings

Northern Plant Lore: A Field Guide to the Ancestral Use of Plants in Northern Europe

The Runes in 9 Minutes

About the Author

Hugh B. Long is an Award Winning Canadian Journalist and Best Selling Author. He writes full time, and is passionate about Science Fiction and Fantasy rooted in Mythology. He also writes Norse and Viking themed non-fiction under the pen name – Eoghan Odinsson.

Graduating from the University of Aberdeen's School of Engineering in Scotland with his Masters of Science degree, he subsequently taught for the University, and was a dissertation advisor for graduate students.

In addition to his academic background, Hugh also holds a Black Belt in Shito-Ryu Karate, a Brown Belt in Budoshin Ju-Jitsu, and was study group leader in D.C. for the Association of Renaissance Martial Arts. (Historical European Martial Arts). Hugh has taught Martial Arts in Canada and the USA.

Hugh recently returned from a 10 year stretch working in the Washington D.C. area, and is now back in his native Ottawa Valley where he lives with his wife, son and two dogs.

www.ingramcontent.com/pod-product-compliance
Lightning Source LLC
Chambersburg PA
CBHW071209130626
46555CB00004B/1641